BEYOND HUMAN

E.B. JAXS

E.B. JAXS

Copyright © 2022 by E.B. JAXS

Beyond Human (Book One)

All Rights Reserved

ISBN: 978-1-64153-430-7

CONTENTS

CHAPTER 1

The missing poster rustled in the breeze, drawing Ben's attention to it again, the face of his oldest friend staring back at him. Was there any point in them still being up? Two months, and still no sign. Blinking, tears threatening again, he stood, stepping over to it. Pulling it down wasn't going to change anything. Paul was gone. No one knew what had happened. He hadn't said anything, although... Ben bit down on his bottom lip.

For a while before, Paul was acting strange. It was something Ben commented on to the police when they were starting their search for Paul, but acting strangely hadn't opened any leads. There was no reason anyone knew of for how he'd been acting. Sighing, Ben raked a hand through his hair, wishing there was something more they could have done.

After spending days out looking for Paul, they had to go back to their normal lives. There was no other choice. He wasn't anywhere to be found. No body either. It was still possible to believe he was alive out there somewhere, but if he was, surely he'd have been in contact. Every day was a case of going through the motions.

"You okay?"

Nodding, Ben turned to look at David. "As okay as I can be." Their eyes met for a moment. "Some days are harder than others."

"I know." David stepped closer, eyes on the poster behind Ben. "The days when it's impossible to pretend he isn't where he's supposed to be." He shook his head. "I keep thinking someone should have found something by now."

"Unless Paul didn't want to be found."

"Do you think it was a choice?"

"With how things are, the lack of evidence, I can't help thinking it's the only possibility now." Ben shrugged. "I remember the police saying Paul didn't take anything with him. His keys, his wallet, and his phone, and he wasn't the kind of person to leave anything behind. If he'd gone out, he'd have taken them unless he had a reason not to."

Silence followed Ben's words. David's eyes stayed on the missing poster, studying Paul's picture as though it was going to give them some answers, before looking at Ben. "We all want there to be a reason, Ben. Paul disappearing... it doesn't make any sense. I don't remember there being any problems, but maybe there were, and we knew nothing about it."

Had it not been for how Paul was acting, Ben would have said there was no possible way he'd be hiding something from them, only he seemed to be doing what he could to put some distance between them. "Did you notice what was happening?" Ben sighed. "How sometimes Paul would act like we weren't friends?"

Breathing a sign of relief, David nodded. "I thought I was the only one who noticed. Normally he'd have come to us if there was a problem, but he didn't. Him not telling us anything... it was unusual."

"We need to start asking why he was trying to keep us at arm's length before he disappeared entirely." Ben ran his tongue over his bottom lip. "I know I am looking for a reason, but this is Paul. Six months without any contact, and no sign of a body, makes me think he's out there somewhere, and he has a reason for hiding."

"Should we tell the police?"

"Are they likely to listen? We're going to them with nothing more than theories, friends talking about something they thought they knew, with the most logical explanation being that we simply didn't know Paul as well as we thought we did. If we're going to learn anything more about what happened, I think we're going to need to do it ourselves."

"You seem to have been thinking about this a lot."

"On the days I miss him the most, I can't help it. Paul wouldn't have left without saying something to me unless there was a good reason not to. We'd been friends since kindergarten."

"Maybe the police are right. Maybe we didn't know him as well as we thought we did. None of us would ever have believed he'd disappear without saying something. Learning you didn't know... I thought if any of us knew where he was, it would be you."

"Yeah, so did I." Ben glanced back at the poster. "I can't keep acting as though everything's okay because it's not, and I have to find him." He shook his head. "I have to try, at least."

***

Knocking on the door to the Hutchinsons' place wasn't the easiest thing to do. Ben stood at the front of the group; decision made he'd be their spokesperson because it was the logical thing to do. He was the one likely leading them into a wild goose chase, so the least he could do was be the parents to enter Paul's room.

Regina opened the door. The shadows under her eyes were a sign she hadn't been sleeping much. For a few seconds, she looked at them before she smiled. "It's really nice to see you all." She stepped back, and they entered the house, Ben gently putting a hand on Regina's shoulder as he passed. "How are you doing?"

"It's been hard." Ben shrugged. "Harder for you, I guess."

"Paul wasn't the kind of person to leave without telling us where he was going. Not taking his phone... well, I thought that detail was more important than the police did; I'm not even sure if they're still looking."

Nodding, Ben raked a hand through his hair. "We were wondering if we could look at his room. I thought Paul leaving his phone behind was weird too, but I wasn't sure if I should bring it up or not. This... nothing makes any sense. Paul disappearing... I know it's been longer than it should have been."

"Of course, it hasn't." Regina's eyes met with Ben's. "You shouldn't have this weight on your shoulders. I know it's not as though you can pretend everything's fine, but you spent over a week searching for him in the early days, and that's more than we could ever have asked for. Paul's disappearance was always going to take time to come to terms with."

"More than anything, I want to try to work out what might have happened. I can't keep pretending; I can live a normal life without my best friend in it."

"Ben..."

"We aren't the police. It's likely we won't find anything. I know it's stupid, but I want to try."

Studying him, teeth buried in her bottom lip, Regina's eyes then moved on to the others. David, Tracey, Sam, and Rebecca, all willing to look more deeply into what happened to Paul because he'd been as important to them as he was to Ben. Leaving it to a police force who didn't seem to care wasn't something they were willing to do.

"If you're that determined, I'm not going to stop you." She smiled. "I understand why you can't give up because I haven't been able to either." She slipped her hand into her pocket, pulling out Paul's phone, which she held out to Ben. "Even though he never had one before, Paul put a lock on the phone. I've been trying to work out what it is. So far, I haven't had any luck."

"What do you think it is?"

"A date. I've put in every date that's ever been important to us, but it's still locked."

***

There didn't seem to be anything out of place other than the fact Paul wasn't there. David was already going through files on Paul's laptop that lock was much simpler to guess than the one on the phone, and Ben couldn't help wondering why the police hadn't got someone to hack into the phone. As they were the ones who were meant to be searching for him, it was their job to find all the evidence.

Important dates hadn't worked. At least the ones Regina knew hadn't worked. She knew all their birthdays, so she'd definitely have tried them. Ben stared down at the screen. There was one important date to all of them, a day they'd never be able to forget, and he tapped in the date Paul disappeared. Even though he hadn't expected it to work, it did.

Blinking, unable to believe it, Ben went to the menu; knowing he needed to be methodical if he was going to learn anything, he had to find what Paul had hidden. First, the messages. Inbox, outbox, and drafts were all empty. Ben leaned back in the chair, staring at the screen. Paul deleted all his messages. Paul never deleted his messages, but he had, which... Ben shook his head.

"What's wrong?" Ben glanced at Rebecca. "You still can't work out the code?"

"No, I have the code. Paul deleted all his messages." Saying the words didn't make it seem any more real. "I think he was worried the wrong person might manage to get into his phone."

Eyebrow raised, Tracey looked at Ben. She was the one who least believed what they were saying; she was there for David rather than Paul. "The wrong person?"

Shrugging, not wanting to argue, Ben turned his attention to the pictures because Paul had hundreds of them. Instead, there was one, a single picture of an old cassette tape. "Okay, the messages being deleted was strange, but this... he deleted every single one of the pictures apart from this one." Ben turned the phone for them to look at it. "It was taken the night before he disappeared."

"A picture of a cassette." Tracey shook her head. "Is that meant to mean something?"

"Maybe. I have no idea. For now, we have a phone Paul seems to have wiped except for one picture. Messages gone, even though he used to say he kept them for the memories. He never wanted to forget the experiences we had. I don't doubt everything else is gone too, and this is our first clue to find him. If we find the tape, it might tell us something we need to know."

Tracey opened her mouth, probably to argue more, but before she could say anything, Sam stood. "It might be nothing. We don't know until we spend some time looking for the cassette."

Rolling her eyes, Tracey did the same. "Fine. I still think this is pointless."

"Yeah, we know what you think." David's voice was flat. "You've told us more than once, Trace. We get it, and you're probably right, but we all want to do more, Paul's our friend."

"Paul was your friend, Dave. I was there because I am your twin." She shrugged, turning her attention to the room. "Okay, we split the room into five, each one of us taking an area, and it should make it easier for us to find the tape if it's here. If it's not, then we at least haven't wasted a lot of time searching for it."

Nodding, Ben gave her a smile. "That's why we like you."

She shook her head, not taking him seriously for a second, but then she'd always believed they accepted her for David. "Bec, can you do the bookcases? Dave can search the desk, as he's already there, and the floor around it. I'll take the chest of drawers and the floor around there. Sam, you're doing the wardrobe; check the pockets of all the clothes. Ben, you're going to do the bed and bedside table. Check every possible place you can."

It wasn't a surprise Ben found nothing, to begin with. All the normal places someone would look were empty. Then he crawled under the bed, looking up at the bed frame, and that was when he saw it. One cassette tape, stuck in the darkest corner possible, something he wouldn't have found unless he was specifically looking. Reaching out with a shaking hand, he pulled it down. When he stood, with it in his hand, the others finally truly believed there was something to his belief that Paul's disappearance was strange.

CHAPTER 2

As the only person who still had a cassette player, Ben's house was where they went next. Regina was happy for them to go, even though she was confused by the tape. It was an unusual place to leave it, but it seemed Paul was trying to hide what he had done from anyone who didn't actually know him, and he knew Ben would be able to listen to the cassette.

Gathering around the hi-fi, something that was older than they were, Ben slipped the cassette into the deck. No one else was home, making it possible for them to listen in peace. First, there was the usual sound of static, as someone prepared to speak to the microphone, and then Paul's voice, something none of them had heard since the day before he disappeared.

"I'm sorry." Paul sighed. "I never wanted to get you involved in this, but if you've found the tape, it's obvious you've made your own choice. The story is longer than I have time to tell. I need to leave before they can do anything to me because I know they'd be willing to harm me to get the book back, and I'm going to do everything I can to protect it. The book can be found at McKaulkin Storage. What I need you to do, if you're willing to help, is get it. Just be careful. They're probably already watching you."

For a while, they listened to the sound of the tape, but there was nothing more. Biting down hard on his lip Ben looked at the others. "Are we willing to help?"

Tracey shook her head. "They're probably already watching us? I don't want anything to do with this. We have no idea what 'the book' is, or why Paul had it, or why he left us a tape to explain all of this."

Ben studied Tracey. "Paul chose to disappear to protect us. To protect his parents. We know he deleted everything off his phone, so they wouldn't have evidence of our lifelong friendships, knowing they'd come looking for us first. He gave up his future for us, and I'm not going to pretend this didn't happen. I'm not going back to school tomorrow without looking for this book. You can make whatever choice you want, but mine was made the moment I found this tape."

"Running into a danger we don't understand." Sam looked at Tracey. "Normally, I'd be the first to argue we should help Paul. But this... it's different. None of us has any knowledge of what Paul was doing before he disappeared, and there's no logical reason for us to be jumping into this without more information."

"How are we going to get it without the book?" Ben sighed. "That will tell us something more."

"Going round in circles will get us nowhere." David looked around the room. "We know Paul did make the decision to leave. He said it was because 'they', whoever they are, want the book back, but none of us knows anything about what this book is. Do we?" Everyone shook their heads. "Paul told us nothing about any of this."

"For the last month, he wasn't hanging out with us." Rebecca raked a hand through her hair. "He was trying to keep his distance, probably because of the book. He didn't want us involved; only then did he come to the conclusion that he didn't have any other choice, probably because he needed to leave suddenly. Not so suddenly, he hadn't planned out how to get a message to us."

"He assumed." Tracey stood. "Paul assumed we would care enough to start looking for him, and when we did, he believed we'd choose to go looking for a book none of us knows anything about, linked to a mysterious 'they'. This sounds like we're getting involved in something we shouldn't be. Something we aren't capable of dealing with."

"You don't need to come." Ben took the tape out of the desk, putting it in his pocket with the phone. "I'm not going to ask anyone to come with me, but I am going to McKaulkin Storage. Paul left this for me, more than for any of you, so I have to go."

"Paul was our friend." David smiled. "I'm going with you, whatever happens."

Breathing deeply, looking more annoyed than anything, Tracey looked at David. "Why do you need to do this?"

David shrugged. "Paul needs our help. I can't walk away from it any more than Ben can. This... knowing he's out there somewhere is enough of a reason for me to find this book. Yeah, it's probably going to be dangerous, and you'd argue it's better for us to stay as far away from this mess as possible. The Likelihood is you're right. Doing this is the stupidest thing any of us could do, but Paul was dealing with it on his own. Now we know what's happening; we can do something to help."

"Obviously, he was doing it on his own because he knew it was dangerous and didn't want us involved." Tracey paced from one side of the room to the other. "Why is it we now make the decision we're going to jump into this when we have no idea what anything is?"

"What would the decision have been before he disappeared?" Rebecca looked at Tracey, and Tracey stared back at her. "If we knew he needed help before he disappeared, what would your answer have been?"

"To get more information."

"You ask that question, and Paul doesn't have an answer for you. He has the book. He knows there are people after him. He can't tell you anything more than that. What's your choice?"

"I don't know." Tracey kept pacing. "I want to help Paul, but he disappeared. He made the decision he was better off far away from here and that… it points to this being far more than any of us are ready for."

"Unfortunately, it does, and it was more than Paul was ready for either." Rebecca smiled. "I know we have a complicated decision to make, but I think we have to try to get the book for Paul. From there, we can work out what the next steps are."

Nodding, Ben looked at Tracey and then Sam. "Jumping into this with the information we have isn't something I'd do under normal circumstances either. The two of you are right to be wary. It's not a simple choice to make, but we have a place to start. I accept we don't know much, and going to somewhere Paul hid a book might end up being dangerous, so I don't want either of you coming if you aren't certain of the choice you're making."

"Ben's right." David sighed. "Paul's decision means it's likely we're walking into something which will cause us all problems in the near future, but if it means he can come home, it's worth the price."

Sam shook his head. "Unless one of us dies."

For a few seconds, all Ben could do was stare at Sam. "Do you think that will happen?"

"As Paul left without a word to any of us, I don't see any reason it's not a possibility. I don't think it's likely if we're careful, but we have to be logical about this. Why would Paul have kept this from all of us otherwise? Why would he have disappeared, deleting everything off his phone, if there wasn't some serious weight to all of this."

"When Paul first disappeared, I thought it was a prank." Tracey stilled, leaning against a wall, fingers tapping against her leg. "He'd reappear in a couple of days, laugh at all of us for being so worried, and we'd move on - only he didn't. The longer this has gone on, the more obvious it's become there's something more to it. Finding the tape... I don't know. This... I don't think we're ready."

"Okay, how about we take a couple of days to think about this?" Ben looked at his friends. "No one knows we have any idea what might have happened to Paul. We can take some time to work through any worries or uncertainties, and then we can go from there."

Rebecca was the first of the group to nod. "I think Ben's right. We aren't going to make a decision right now. Giving ourselves some time is the best thing we can do. I know what I want to do. I know what I believe I should do. That doesn't mean I'm not terrified at the very thought. Plus, it will give us some time to come up with a workable plan to get into a storage unit we don't have a key for."

"Paul didn't leave us much to go on." Ben nibbled his bottom lip. "I'll start working out a plan."

***

Scrolling through the contacts on Paul's phone, all their numbers were deleted, Ben didn't see any unusual numbers. It was entirely family, as though Paul didn't have any friends at all. He was trying to wipe them from his life, his way of protecting them from whatever he'd found himself in the middle of; only in doing so, he'd made it much harder for them to find the answers they needed.

What was the book? How did Paul get hold of it? Ben raked a hand through his hair, going back to his own phone. There were texts from Paul during a couple of months before he disappeared, but as Ben went through the days, it was obvious they were becoming rarer, and he remembered a couple of days before he went missing when Paul wasn't at school. No one knew where he was. When Ben texted to check-in, there were no responses. Was Paul preparing for what came next?

There was no way to know without finding Paul, and finding Paul seemed to mean finding the book. Sighing, Ben turned back to the map in front of him. According to the map, McKaulkin Storage was on the outskirts of town, somewhere they'd need a car to get to, which meant they needed Tracey with them. So far, she was the only one who'd passed her driving test.

If Tracey didn't agree... Ben shook his head. A problem to solve if it did exist. The one question they did have was how they got the key for the storage facility. Did one of them pretend to be Paul? If he'd ever been there, it would lead to complicated questions. Why hadn't he left a key if he wanted them to get the book? Was the key something they'd missed? Unless... Ben turned back to his messages, reading through everything Paul sent up until the day he went missing.

Nothing there to point him at the key. Nothing on the tape, other than more static. Ben shook his head. There had to be something they missed. Paul, as far as Ben knew, didn't keep any kind of journal, but there was one place to look for anything they might need - Paul's locker. If, as he'd said, he'd disappeared before he was truly ready, then there was a chance he'd left something there.

At least he had another step to take. Ben pulled the map closer to him, sketching a couple of possible routes onto it. They'd probably need one route in and one route back, with the route back being one that didn't lead them to any of their houses. Maybe it would be best to head to the school first before splitting up to walk home. Of course, it would mean Tracey leaving her car behind, something she might not be willing to do. It was the easiest way to keep them all safe if there really was something to worry about. Keeping his friends safe was always going to be his main priority.

CHAPTER 3

Walking up to Paul's locker, Ben put in the code he knew almost as well as his own. The two of them borrowed each other's lockers all the time, up until the point Paul started to pull away from them. Opening it, he wasn't entirely surprised to find it appeared to be entirely empty. From the looks of things, there was nothing left, but he thought about the first tape and Paul's decision to hide it. Running his fingers around the inside of the locker, he tried to find what might have been left.

Hidden at the very top of the locker, right by the door, was a key. Someone who wasn't looking for it definitely wouldn't have found it. Breathing a sigh of relief, Ben pulled the tape off it, and when he looked at it, he knew it was for a padlock, likely the one on the storage unit the book was in. One problem solved. Now all he had to do was get through a couple of days pretending everything was normal.

Slipping the key into his pocket Ben closed the locker, walking away from it. Everyone else was too busy to notice him, focused on their own normal lives, a position he'd been in two months earlier. None of them thought about Paul on a daily basis. Most of them didn't think of him at all. He hadn't been their friend. He wasn't someone they noticed was missing every day.

It was definitely easier that way. Ben walked down the corridor, eyes meeting with David's for a second. None of them had talked about what was going to happen next. Two days felt like a long time to wait, but it made sense. It was a chance to make plans, to think through all the possibilities, and then work out the best way of doing what Paul asked them to do. Get the book. Hopefully, once they had the book, they'd have an idea of what to do next.

At least there was still school to focus on, to take his mind off everything. Ben headed to geography, a class he shared with Rebecca, who was already there when he reached their table. As he sat down, she looked at him. He smiled, and she smiled back. Then she looked at the book in front of her, teeth buried in her bottom lip.

"Did you find it?"

Ben blinked. "Find what?"

"The key."

"You think I was looking for it?"

"Paul was your best friend. If anyone knew where to look, it was you."

Nodding, Ben double checked to make sure it was still where he put it. "We have what I believe is the key."

"Good." She turned to him again. "How are you feeling about all of this?"

"Confused, mostly. I keep thinking back to before he disappeared and how distant he'd become because I feel like I should have done more to get him to open up."

"He obviously didn't want to talk to us about any of this." She raked a hand through her hair. "I get it. He thought he was keeping us safe, but by doing what he did, he's made this all much more complicated than it needs to be."

"Are you sure about finding the book?" He studied her, the quietest member of the group who always seemed to be a little distant from the rest of them. "Tracey and Sam are worried for the right reasons."

"I know they are, but not going is letting Paul down, and I'm not willing to do that."

"With everything that's happened, I kinda feel like Paul let us down." He looked down at the table rather than at Rebecca. She wasn't normally the person Ben would open up to, but Paul was gone, and she seemed more understanding than he had realized before. "If he'd been open with us, we wouldn't be where we are now."

Nodding, Rebecca put her hand on Ben's arm. "I get it. Last night I felt the same way. The message he left us was short, telling us nothing about what we were getting involved in, and as he disappeared, it could only be bad. Now... I keep thinking about what it might be. What did Paul find? I think the mystery of it helped me to set aside some of the annoyance I felt. I want to learn for me too. Is what he found something that will change the world?"

***

Tracey almost always spent lunches alone in the art room. Ben found himself stopping by, something he'd never normally have done. As he stepped into the room, she looked back at him. For a few seconds, their eyes met before she turned her attention to the piece she was working on, a barely-there sketch he knew would become something amazing.

"You wanted to see if I'd made a decision yet."

Ben shook his head. "No, Trace, I wanted to check to see how you're doing." He walked toward her. "I know what we've learnt is complicated, but even before all of this, it was hard. Paul's disappearance hit all of us."

Shrugging, Tracey focused on the sketch. "Paul was always the best one for putting my mind at ease when I felt most like an outsider. That I was accepted for me, and not only because I was Dave's twin sister." She shook her head. "After all these years, it doesn't entirely make sense to have doubts still, but occasionally I still wonder if we'd ever have been friends if it wasn't for Dave. He was the outgoing one."

"Maybe we wouldn't have got to know each other." Ben smiled. "Dave is the reason we had a chance to break through that shy shell of yours all those years ago. He isn't the reason we became friends with you. You're the reason for that." He stepped closer enough to put his hand on her shoulder. "If we'd not become friends with you as you were, then we wouldn't pretend."

"Paul said something similar." Tracey sighed. "I miss him, Ben, and I just... I understand why you want to look for him, why you want to find the book. Last night I wasn't kind about any of this, and I'm sorry. I should have been more understanding, but there was a moment when I felt like there might be hope, only for it to be taken away. The book... we don't know anything about it. Anything about why Paul had it or why he disappeared because of it.

"I keep thinking maybe it was nothing. Maybe Paul was paranoid; there was something he believed was happening that wasn't because it makes more sense than people being after him because he found a book. Only there was a text he sent me a couple of nights before he disappeared." She put the pencil down and pulled her phone out of her pocket. "It didn't seem to be anything at the time, but now I can't help wondering."

When she held the phone out to him, Ben took it, and Tracey watched him as he read the short text. 'Miss you. I know I've been distant recently. I'm sorry. Things will either get easier soon, or they're going to fall apart entirely.'

The text was definitely Paul's style. He didn't do shortening words unless he had no other option. Ben ran his tongue over his bottom lip. "Fall apart entirely?"

"Of course, I thought it was something to do with school. I thought he'd been busy working on a project." Tracey shook her head. "Technically, he was working on a project, but it was nothing to do with school."

"No, it wasn't." Ben sighed. "He never said anything to the rest of us."

"He probably sent it to me because I wasn't going to ask questions. The last thing he wanted was for one of us to become involved in this mess." She studied Ben. "Until he felt like he had no other option when things did fall apart entirely, and again I wonder how much of this is real. How much of it was in his head."

"Finding out the answer to that question does mean going to the storage unit. I found the key in Paul's empty locker, so we have everything we need. I've been working out routes, planning out how to keep us safe, and I think we should be able to do this."

"Ben…"

"I'm not going to push you into anything. You still have time to make a decision." He handed her phone back. "We don't know what we're walking into. Maybe we'll find you were right, and this was all in Paul's head. The problem is we won't know until we go."

Nodding, Tracey slipped her phone back into her pocket. "We won't. Okay, maybe I'll come if only so I can say I told you so."

***

Sam was in Ben's last class of the day, sitting in their usual spot. Normally it was the three of them, Paul sitting on the other side of the table, him not being there was strange. Ben took his seat, glancing at Sam. Sam was focusing on writing something down. When he was finished, he looked at Ben, their eyes meeting for a second.

"Last night, I found myself researching Paul's case." Sam shook his head. "It's stupid, but I wanted to see what the police said before about all of this, trying to work out if there really was something we should be looking into."

"Tracey told you her theory."

E.B. Jaxs

"Yeah, she did, and I wanted to look into it more deeply. Everything about the way he acted pointed to there being something wrong. None of us pried, giving him time to work through whatever the problem was. We checked in every so often, and when I saw him in class, I didn't think there was anything wrong with his mental health, although when he left school, things were different.

"I noticed him getting into a car one afternoon. Even though I knew both his parent's cars, it wasn't one I recognized. Turns out it was his uncle's, at least according to his mom, so I can't help wondering if maybe his uncle was involved in this somehow. We might want to give him a call to see if he can tell us anything more about it."

"Why didn't you say anything before?"

"Honestly, Ben, I didn't have a reason to. After I checked in with Paul's mom, I thought his uncle was probably giving him a lift. The fact he was looking around could easily be explained by him looking for the car. Everything had a logical explanation at the time, and I didn't think about it being linked to Paul's mental health until Tracey brought it up. She does make a good point."

"She does, and I'm not going to say she's wrong. For now, we don't know what any of this is. Like I said last night, I'm not willing to push anyone into doing this if they'd rather keep out of it."

29

"Only, if this is something, then there's a chance we don't have an option anymore. We know about the book. All it takes is for one of us to go, and all of us are in danger. Unlike Paul, we had no reason to keep our distance from each other. They know we're friends if they exist, so if you and David go, then it's not only the two of you they'll come after."

Nodding, he raked a hand through his hair. "I hadn't thought about it like that."

"Understandable." Sam smiled. "It's either all of us, or it's none of us. The more I think about it, the more inclined I am to go, however dangerous it might end up being."

CHAPTER 4

They gathered around the table. Ben looked at the map he'd been sketching routes on, going over them all again in his head. There was nothing easy about what they planned to do if Paul was being honest about the situation he'd found himself in. However, there was an equal chance they were simply going along with his delusions.

"We're all going?" Ben lifted his eyes. Rebecca was the first to nod, her decision having been made the first afternoon, followed by the rest. "In that case, we need to be ready for what might happen. Paul left the key for us in his locker." He bit down on his bottom lip. "The way it was cleared out shows he was preparing to leave before it happened. He might not have had as much time as he hoped, but he was always planning on leaving and doing it without saying a word to any of us about what was happening."

"He didn't want us in danger." Rebecca shrugged. "As painful as it is to have found out the truth, it's better he didn't. Had we known anything, there's a chance we might not have been able to do anything now." Her eyes met with Ben's. "We're better positioned to be able to help him if the book is real, and if not, we can go to his parents. Tell them we believe this all has something to do with what Paul had come to believe."

"I agree with Becca." Tracey nodded. "We need to find out whether or not the book is real before we decide what our next steps are. The likelihood is it's not, but this is a situation where we need to learn the truth. Paul's parents knowing might make it easier for the police to find him. They'll be able to look for him in a different way if they know he believes he needs to hide from someone."

"Okay, then we need to be ready for the possibility he was telling the truth." Ben gestured at the map. "Someone could be watching us right now. I don't know how much I believe what Paul said, but I can't pretend I didn't hear the fear in his voice. He was scared. It was real fear, whether or not the book was real, which is more than enough of a reason for me to take the possibility of something happening to us seriously. What I want is for us all to be safe.

"Hence the map. We take one route to the storage unit, and we take another one back. All those routes take us to the school rather than to any of our houses because that way we can split up." He looked at Tracey. "I have no reason to believe it won't be

E.B. Jaxs

safe at school for a few hours before you can come back to pick it up. From there, we go to our houses."

"As only one of us will have the book, they won't know who to go to first." Sam raked a hand through his hair. "Ben, will you be the person taking the book?"

"Possibly. I don't know how much they could already have looked into Paul. With a little research, they'd have learnt we became friends in kindergarten, so I'd be the most likely to keep the book. That..." Ben shrugged. "I think Rebecca might be the best option. You're the one who became friends with us the latest and had, to most, the least connection to Paul."

Rebecca ran her tongue over her bottom lip. "I can see that." She breathed in deeply. "If everyone agrees, then I'll take the book and keep it safe."

"Good." Ben looked around the table again. "Any arguments against it being Becca?" He breathed a mental sigh of relief when everyone shook their heads. "Then we have that decision made." Pulling the laptop closer, he showed them the image of McKaulkin Storage. "Now we have the next issue. We don't know which one of the units is Paul's. We have a key that fits into a padlock, and that... well, we're going to need to search the place for the right padlock."

"Well, we have a brand name." The key was on the table with everything else, and Sam picked it up, studying it. "What does that tell us?"

"Nothing amazingly useful. The brand makes a number of padlocks, and some of them have very similar-looking keys. From what I can tell, most of those padlocks happen to be the bestsellers, which makes it likely there are going to be a number of them, and we may well end up opening the wrong padlock." Ben sighed. "Unless we learn something more, it's going to be guesswork."

David gestured for Ben to pass the laptop over. "We should be able to learn something more. The unit would have needed to be rented by someone. In order to find it, we're going to need a name. Paul wouldn't have been able to rent one himself, making it much more likely it was someone older, and Sam said before about Paul's uncle picking him up. Do we have a name for the uncle we can search for?"

The whole time David was talking, he was tapping away on the keyboard. Out of all of them, he was the one with the best tech skills, and Ben let him do whatever he was doing while he went back through Paul's phone, looking at the contacts. As expected, when he reached 'Uncle', there were three different names, and none of them had surnames.

"Even though it's likely the best route we can take, I'm not getting anything useful from the phone. Three uncles, and no idea whether they're maternal or paternal."

"We can check all variations, Ben. It'll take a little longer, but there's no reason to give up yet. Do we know what Regina's maiden name is?"

"Jackson, I think."

"We'll start with Hutchinson and go from there." David raked a hand through his hair. "First uncle's name?"

"Thomas."

After a few seconds, David shook his head. "No sign of a Thomas Hutchinson, and no sign of a Thomas Jackson. No Tom for either of those names. Do we have any other shortened versions for Tom?"

"Thom." David looked at Rebecca. "T H O M, not T O M."

"Yeah, I'm an idiot." He tapped that in. "Still nothing."

"Tommy? Or spelt with an ie." Tracey scrolled through her phone. "He might also have gone for Maas, which is a Dutch diminutive. Then, of course, we have all the different variations on spelling. Even though it's spelt one way in the phone, there's a chance they went for a different spelling at the McKaulkin, in case they were found by someone else."

"Good point." David sighed. "Write them all down for me, Trace, and I'll go through them. Then we can do the same for the other two uncles."

"Looks like Regina's maiden name is Jackson. I checked the register for local marriages, and that's what came up." Rebecca looked at Ben. "Give me another name, and I'll start searching for spelling variations."

"Give me the third, and I'll do the same. The sooner we get through this, the better." Sam picked up his phone. "Hopefully, this won't take as long as I think it will."

"Oh, it will." Ben sighed. "The second uncle is Alex, which could be short for Alexander, and then we have the third uncle Michael. Neither of which have a small number of variations."

David looked at Ben, eyebrow raised. "There, I was hoping I'd got the easy task."

"Nothing about any of this is going to be easy, David." Ben smiled. "I'm sorry."

"Yeah, so am I."

For what felt like hours, David tapped away at the keyboard, trying out different variations of the names they had for the three uncles. "Got it. Finally." He breathed in deeply. "The unit is under the name Mykolas Jackson. Michael didn't want it to be easy to find. We're looking for unit number 213."

Ben nodded, scrawling the number down in his notebook. "Okay, so we have a unit to look at, and now we need to decide how we're going to do this. Do we all go to the unit? Should only a couple go?"

"Whatever you decide, I'll stay in the car." Tracey leaned back in her chair. "If anything unusual happens, it'll make it easier for all of us. That way, I can leave as fast as we need to go."

"Okay, that makes sense." Ben looked at David. "The two of us go, leave Sam and Becca to keep an eye out, and then if they see anything, they can let us know?"

"Unless we split up. Make them think, if they are watching, we need to look for the unit." Rebecca shrugged. "I feel like we need to misdirect them. They don't know what we know. We don't know that they know. The more careful we are, the simpler this is going to be." She looked down at the map. "I kinda wish we had two drivers right about now. That would make this a lot easier, rather than us all going in Tracey's car."

"You're taking this very seriously, Becca."

"Why wouldn't I be? We have two options - Paul is delusional, or he was telling the truth. If he was telling the truth, I'd rather prepare for that because not preparing for that is how we end up dead or, in some government facility, being asked questions we can't answer. That means we do the best things we can to keep us safe."

"Becca reads a lot of thrillers." Tracey smiled at Rebecca. "Right now, they appear to be coming in very handy."

Rebecca shrugged. "It's better to prepare rather than simply walk into a situation we don't understand blind. We know where we're going. I think as you've all decided I'm keeping the book, I should grab it and hide it." She ran her tongue over her bottom lip. "When we open one of the units, they'll likely notice."

"Unless we're careful." Ben looked at the image of McKaulkin Storage once more. "If you go straight there, they'll be watching you more closely. Take a more roundabout route; look like you're checking all the padlocks as you go past because they don't know what we know."

"Might also be worth taking some bolt cutters." Sam shrugged as Ben turned to him. "They don't know we have the key. It's best for us to look like we're going there to check it out, have the bolt cutters there just in case. None of us wants to break into a unit, but we have limited options, and if we open a few of them...."

"We're going to draw attention we don't need." David shook his head. "We misdirect, but we don't cause any trouble; we don't have to. Taking the bolt cutters isn't something I'm against, but we don't damage anything, especially as there's going to be CCTV. We do what needs to be done, and then we leave." He ran his tongue over his bottom lip. "What do we know about the place."

"According to this, it's open 24 hours, so we can go after sunset, making it harder for them to see us. There's likely not going to be anyone on the gate at that point, which probably means we're going to need a code."

"Two minutes." Another few taps on the keyboard. "I have the code."

"Okay, good. We go in, and we move fast, but we don't make it obvious we know exactly where the unit is. Each one of us looks in a different direction. Becca..."

"I'm going to head to a bus stop once I have the book. They're more likely to follow the car because taking the book on the bus is the most stupid decision anyone could make, and that's exactly why I should."

CHAPTER 5

The sun was setting as they drove toward McKaulkin Storage. Ben found himself glancing in the rear view mirror more often than he thought he would, watching for anyone who might be following them. He couldn't see anyone, but that didn't necessarily mean they weren't there, something he knew that pointed to his worries and getting the better of him. Was it the same for Paul? Did he spend all his time watching out for someone who might be following him?

At least Ben wasn't the only one. They all seemed to be doing something similar, worried about the same thing. Even Tracey. Unfortunately, crossing town to get to where they needed to be was going to take time. It was possible they might be found at any point. Sighing, he raked a hand through his hair before feeling Rebecca's hand on his arm.

"Whatever happens, everything will be okay." Her voice was reassuring. "No matter how hard it might be, we'll find a way to deal with this."

"How can you be so calm?"

"Nothing we do will change how things are. Paul has disappeared. This is our chance to learn something more, even though none of us has any idea whether or not the book is real, and either way, we'll have an answer to that question. From there, we can only deal with things as they happen."

Slowly, Ben nodded. "I know. This is just... I never thought anything like this was possible."

"Our lives might be changed for good. They might not." Rebecca shrugged. "I feel like right now we're at the point where it can be either, and we're as prepared as we can be for whatever might happen next. There's a chance none of this is real. Paul left us a tape sending us here for no reason, and he somehow managed to rent a storage unit in the name of an uncle who knew nothing about any of this."

"Do you think it was a delusion?"

"I honestly have no idea, Ben. From the interactions I had with Paul, few though they were, I wouldn't have said it was, but there are those who are very good at hiding what they're going through."

Paul could easily be one of those people. He might have disappeared, believed he was being searched for by 'them', leaving breadcrumbs to follow for anyone who knew him well enough to be able to find them. In the end, that was likely to be

Ben, as he was the one who understood how Paul thought, making it relatively simple to work out how to get into the phone. The next steps might end up being more complicated.

Until they reached the McKaulkin they'd have no way of knowing one way or another. It was simply going to be a case of waiting to see what happens next. Going over it all in his head wasn't something he could stop himself from doing as they drove toward the true beginning of learning what happened to Paul.

***

No one was there when they arrived, something they expected to be the case, and the gates were locked with a code. David was the one who jumped out of the car to tap it in, and slowly the gates in front of them opened. From the map, there were a few entrances to McKaulkin. They'd used one relatively close to where the unit was, if they had managed to find the right one. What they wanted to do was make things as simple as possible. If someone was following them, they'd need a quick way out.

Tracey, as planned, didn't leave the car. Ben watched Rebecca for a second, worried about her more than anyone else. She was the one putting her safety on the line to find out if the book actually existed. It was likely there was nothing they could do to talk her out of it. They all knew once she'd made a decision, that was it. She wasn't going to change her mind.

Ben went through the units, focused on keeping up the act. He needed to seem like he was searching for a specific unit. It was when he was halfway down the first lot he heard the sound of a car. Was it Tracey? Whoever it was drove slowly, seeming like they were still outside the gate. Ignoring it as best he could, he kept moving.

Not knowing what Rebecca was doing, where she was, was the hardest part. Focusing on the units, looking at padlocks, he kept up the act in case someone was watching him, emotions swirling. If the book wasn't real, then he was paranoid about everything for no reason. If the book was real, what was their next step going to be? Paul had to leave his entire life behind. Would they all have to do the same thing? Had he dragged them into something truly dangerous?

One foot in front of the other. Looking at a padlock, and then another. There was no other option. It was a decision they'd made together. Crossing from one row to the next, Ben looked to see if there was anyone else around. He could hear three sets of footsteps, exactly what he expected to hear, but that didn't mean there wasn't someone else around. All they needed was quiet shoes.

Shaking his head at himself, Ben turned his attention back to the units. Keep up the act. There was probably no one there, but if there was, what he was doing would hopefully be enough to keep them from thinking they knew exactly where the unit was. Looking at the doors, it seemed unlikely one of them being opened would draw attention.

Right when he was beginning to think they'd made the journey there for no reason, Ben heard something. Footsteps maybe. Holding his breath for a second, he listened more closely, wondering if it might be one of the group, but there was nothing. His imagination. Rather than thinking too much about it, he kept going. It wouldn't be too much longer before Rebecca got to the unit, grabbed whatever was inside of it, and left.

Breathing in deeply, Ben kept moving. Left, right, left, right, and look at another padlock. It felt pointless until he heard the sound of someone behind him. Glancing back, he wasn't surprised to see no one was there. Whoever they were didn't want him to know he was. They needed to move fast because someone had found them.

When his phone vibrated in his pocket, Ben didn't bother to look at it. Instead, he kept moving down the row before heading toward where Tracey's car was. Reaching it, he found the engine was already on, Tracey tapping her fingers on the steering wheel, and when she saw him, she breathed a very obvious sigh of relief. Someone else was there. Although he wanted it to be his imagination, it wasn't the case.

"According to Becca, there was definitely someone near her. She texted me when she heard them to let me know I needed to be ready. Get in the car. I'll be leaving as soon as the others get here."

Nodding, Ben got in the back, taking the same position he'd had before. Rebecca picked the spot she had because it was harder for someone to notice if she was missing that way. "They shouldn't be long. We had everything planned out. All we need to do now is get to the school."

***

Ignoring the planned route, Tracey ducked into an alleyway. From there, she turned down a couple of other alleyways, seeming almost as though she knew exactly what she was doing before she parked, turning off the lights. They all waited. There was nothing else they could do. Someone was following them in a black car with darkened lights, making it harder to see them.

Maybe it would have been better to go to McKaulkin during the day. At least then, they might have been able to hide in traffic. When they were one of the few cars out, it was harder to hide. Yet when the black car didn't appear again, it seemed like they hadn't been found. Tracey's eyes met with Ben's in the rear view.

"Getting to the school from here shouldn't be too complicated, but as I've lost them, it's likely to be easier for me to get home. I can put the car in the garage when I get there. Anyone knocks on the door, and I can pretend I have no idea what they're talking about." She breathed in deeply. "If the rest of you go from here, it'll be better. Someone pulls me over. I can pretend I was out for a drive."

Nodding, Ben did exactly that, with Sam and David doing the same thing. They watched as Tracey drove away before Ben looked at David. "We all need to take different routes home." He raked a hand through his hair. "Becca said she'd called when she got home, although I know she was planning on doing that the long way."

"Something she could be doing for no reason." Sam raked a hand through his hair. "I can go south from here, take the shortest route home."

"Okay, that works." Ben sighed. "Do you really think the car following us was nothing?"

Rather than answering, Sam shrugged, walking away. Ben and David shared a look. "This isn't easy for any of us, Ben. Until today it was possible to think this was nothing, but obviously, it isn't, and the book, whatever it is, is real."

"I know." Ben smiled. "I'll take my normal route home from school, which will leave you to head east, taking a slightly different route to Tracey. When Becca calls, I'll let you know what she says."

"Be careful."

Watching David for a few seconds, Ben breathed in deeply. His heart was pounding hard in his chest, emotions swirling because it was real. Paul wasn't delusional. All he could do was wait until Rebecca called, and then they could start planning on what the next steps were going to be. Whoever was following them couldn't know for certain they'd been able to find the book. They simply assumed it happened.

Going down streets he'd walked a hundred times before; Ben felt less comfortable than he'd ever done before. He kept watch for any unusual cars. Fortunately, there was nothing other than the sounds that seemed like they were cars. When they ended up being nothing, he shook his head at himself, beginning to understand the reason Paul disappeared.

They didn't know where Paul was. If they did, it was likely they'd be after him, not following his friends around in the hope they might have an idea. Considering everything, it seemed more likely they assumed one of them knew where he was. He was more important to them than anything else other than the book.

Finally, after what felt like hours, Ben reached the door to his house. Slipping the key into the front door, he glanced behind him, checking for anyone who might be following him. On the other side of the road was a car he'd seen a couple of times before. A car he hadn't paid much attention to because it seemed like all the other parked cars, but for the first time, he saw there was someone inside it. Someone who happened to be watching the house.

Rather than making a big deal of it, Ben acted as normally as he could, like the glance was nothing more than him checking to make sure no one else had come back at the same time. Then he pushed the door open, stepping into a house he no longer felt safe in, however unlikely it was they'd be making their move any time soon. It was obvious they were waiting for the moment Paul broke character, going back to see one of his friends. Fortunately, they knew nothing about the tape.

CHAPTER 6

Every thirty seconds, Ben checked his phone to make certain he hadn't missed a call. It was almost midnight. Rebecca had to get home soon. He raked a hand through his hair, knowing he needed to be patient because the whole plan was to make certain no one knew she'd found anything. If they found out about the book, things were only going to get more complicated.

Just as he put it down again, promising himself he wasn't going to check it again, it rang, and Ben answered without looking to see who it was. "I'm home." Rebecca sounded tired. "Someone did follow me to the bus stop and onto the first bus. They were trying to act normally, even though it was obvious to me what they were doing wasn't normal, so I took a couple of extra buses. I also stopped off to get a hot chocolate, slipping out through the back when I had it."

"I'm so sorry."

"You have nothing to apologize for. What's happening isn't your fault." She breathed in deeply. "The unit was empty apart from a book and another cassette. Probably another message from Paul. Hopefully, it'll explain how he ended up getting involved in this. I'll give it to you when I see you tomorrow. For now, I need to get some sleep."

"Of course. Sleep well."

"Night, Ben."

Rebecca hung up, and Ben dialed David's number. "Becca's home."

"Good. I was beginning to get worried."

"So was I." Ben raked a hand through his hair. "She was being followed. It might mean they know something about the book."

David sighed. "When I got back, I noticed there was a car watching the house. I called Sam, and he saw the same thing. The car's been there on and off since Paul disappeared, which means they'd been watching us since then, waiting for something to happen. I don't know what."

Nodding, Ben leaned back, resting against the wall. "Same here. Unfortunately. I think they're waiting for Paul to miss us enough to break, but I don't think it's going to happen."

"Paul going through this alone... at least we have each other. We can work through this together. I wish he'd turned to us rather than making the decision to do it all himself."

"Knowing him, he thought it was for the best. We were never going to agree once we learnt the whole truth." Ben shook his head. "All we can do now is see what happens next. Becca said there was a tape with the book, so we'll hopefully get another message from Paul. From there, we're going to need to decide what to do."

"Why would Paul keep the book? I keep asking myself that. There has to be a reason for the decision, even though I have no idea what it might be."

"Yeah, there does, and hopefully, we'll get the explanation tomorrow. Otherwise, all we can do is guess."

"I know. We should both get some sleep for school tomorrow, however hard it might be. Night, Ben."

"Night, David."

As David hung up, Ben turned to Paul's phone. The uncle who'd rented the unit might be involved enough to be able to answer some questions, but there was an equal chance Paul pretended to be his uncle in order to rent the unit rather than the uncle being involved. Getting advice from someone else was tempting, only there was no way to know who was trustworthy, and Paul's uncle might not be.

Putting both phones on the bedside table, Ben turned out the light. He did need to sleep. School was still somewhere he had to go daily, however pointless it seemed. Unfortunately for his chances, his mind was whirring. He stared at the ceiling, wondering what the book was. How did Paul get it? Why were people looking for him and the book? Getting the answers to them was something that might happen when they listened to the tape.

They had a way to get answers, so there was no reason to keep going over everything, yet controlling his mind wasn't an easy task. Ben tried to turn it to anything else, but every time it went back to the book. To wondering how Paul had found it, where it came from and why it existed in the first place? Eventually, he had to have fallen asleep because his alarm woke him up. However, the sleep felt so short.

***

Rebecca put the tape into Ben's hand. Their eyes met for a moment before she went down the hall. Neither of them were in the same class for the day, so her dropping the tape off early was the best thing she could do. He put it into both his pockets, one holding the other tape and one holding Paul's phone. Having them all together was the most logical thing to do.

Going through the motions through the day was complicated. Ben couldn't turn his mind to lessons that felt pointless, and he found himself thinking about Paul again. How had Paul managed to keep pretending? Even though he had the book in his possession, he kept going to school every day until he couldn't any longer. Then again, it was likely his grades were dropping, his lack of interest showing there, but none of them knew anything about it.

The last class of the day was a relief. Art. It wasn't necessary to think too much then, and Ben was able to use his sketches to keep his mind off things he shouldn't be thinking about. They'd get answers soon enough. The plan was to head straight to his place, where the cassette player waited for them, where they'd hopefully learn what else Paul knew about the book.

When the bell rang, Ben looked at the sketched to find he'd drawn images of books. He had no idea what the book Paul found looked like, so there were ornate ones along with more boring ones, and Ben tore it into pieces, dropping it into the bin before he walked out the room. If anyone wanted to try to piece it together, they could because it wouldn't tell them anything useful.

Sighing, Ben walked through the halls to where his friends gathered at the main door. None of them said anything as they left, going straight to Tracey's car, the decision made without them needing to speak. It was a relief when she parked outside. The car was still watching the house, but Ben ignored it. Whoever was sitting there had seen the group enter the house multiple times in the past. What they were doing wasn't unusual in any way.

Once they were safely in the house, Ben stepped over to the hi-fi. Putting the tape into the deck, he waited as the sound of static filled the room before there was Paul's voice. "Okay, you chose to get the book, and I really don't know how to feel about that. I guess it was inevitable. I'm sorry. You should never have been a part of this, but I had limited options when I realized I was being watched." He breathed in deeply. "First thing to know is you need to keep the book hidden. I have no reason to think you haven't already realized that. I just... it's been a long couple of months.

"Leaving was the logical option. They knew I had the book, and they were going to keep watching until I made a mistake. Now they're going to be watching you. Even though I tried to keep you out of this, they know you're my friends. They're going to ask questions at some point, wanting answers you can't know, which is the point when you have to make a decision yourselves."

"You have questions, and I'll do my best to answer them. There's a chance I might miss some. If I do, they'll be someone to help you. All you need to do is text them. They're under Michael on my phone. My uncle's name is actually Tim. We hid the truth because he knew they'd be watching me closely.

"Back before I was involved, Tim was the one who came across the book. I can't tell you anything more than that. It's Tim's story to share. My part started when Tim needed somewhere to hide the book, and he didn't think they knew anything about me. Tim's been distant from the family for a while. We see him every so often at big family gatherings, meaning I was his best option, although he didn't think I'd start trying to learn more."

"That was my big mistake. I'm not the most skilled at hacking. They learnt someone was looking into things they shouldn't be. I knew then I didn't have many other options, so I contacted Tim. We planned out what I'd do if I did need to disappear. On the day they first asked me a few questions, it was obvious they believed I had the book. Then I knew I needed to get out."

"My last night, we did everything we could to hide my trail from anyone who might be able to find it, apart from Ben. He was the one I trusted to learn the answers I had to give. Fortunately, he did find those answers, which means I won't need to head back to town because the town is more dangerous for me than anywhere else right now. I'm safe where I am. Eventually, we will see each other again."

"Hopefully, by then, I'll have answers to the rest of your questions. I know you want me to tell you what the book is, but we don't know. What I do know is that it's locked, and the key is hidden, somewhere we haven't yet learnt about. That's your task. You need to find out where the key is, so we can get into the book."

"Tim believes it links to something that happened many years ago certain departments within the government covered up. He could be right, but until we find the key, we have no way of knowing. Those departments were the ones I tried to hack, something I should have turned to David for, only I didn't want to drag any of you into this. I tried to do it alone, which was my greatest mistake. I'm sorry for keeping this from you. I'm sorry you're involved."

"Now that's done, I don't think I have anything more I can tell you. The rest is up to you. Find the key. Learn the answers we need. Until we have them, we have no idea what we can do next, but for now, they don't know you have the book. They believe I took it with me, as we managed to make a copy of it, although my copy doesn't have anything within."

"Good luck. Hopefully, it won't be too long before we do see each other. I miss you all. Be careful. Anything happens, text Tim."

Static followed the last words, and Ben let it play for a few minutes before accepting there was nothing else on the tape. Ejecting it from the deck, he turned to his friends. They'd found themselves with something someone within the government wanted. Not exactly what they wanted to be doing, yet it wasn't much of a surprise.

"Well, that told us something."

Rebecca nodded. "The book is locked. From what I could tell, it appears to be very old, and that..." She raked a hand through her hair. "The lock is one we couldn't pick because it needs three keys, not one."

Ben studied her. "Paul said we needed to find a key."

"I know, but he was wrong. I couldn't sleep last night, so I spent a lot of time studying the book, and there are three locks. Someone who hadn't spent the time I did on it probably wouldn't have noticed because they're very well hidden."

CHAPTER 7

Pulling the book out from under her bed, Rebecca looked at Ben. It was bigger than he thought it was going to be, thick and almost too big for Rebecca to hide within her jacket, but somehow she managed it. The task she'd taken upon herself was far larger than the task any of the rest of them had. She gave him a smile.

"From the beginning, we knew nothing about this was going to be simple. When I found the book... honestly, I was half hoping Tracey was right. This would have all been much simpler if Paul was delusional. Unfortunately for us, he wasn't. Whatever he got himself involved in was real."

"Are you sure you want to keep it?"

"No, but I'm sure I don't want it to be in anyone else's hands. I'm the logical choice. You're going to be the first person they go to, and from there, it will go down the list to me. By the time they reach me, we'll already be out of here."

"Becca..."

"For now, we're a step ahead. We need to stay a step ahead. Someone wants this enough they're willing to watch over school children." Rebecca shrugged. "David's already working on learning more about the book and where the keys might be. Tracey was the one who did all the driving. You have the tape deck. This is how I'm being useful." She stood, lifting the book onto her bed. "You're welcome to look at it, see if you can find any answers. I didn't, but I'm pretty sure we can't do anything else without those keys."

Running his fingers over the book Ben thought of the sketches he'd done. None of them were close to how ornate the cover of the book was. There was no title on it to tell them anything about it. Instead, it was simply covered with beautiful scrolling, which looked like it might be made from gold, which was more than enough of a reason for people to be searching for it.

"Got any idea what it is?"

"Expensive." Rebecca ran her tongue over her bottom lip. "You know as well as I do how much that could be worth if it is gold, although I'm hoping it isn't. Other than that, I know as much as everyone else, other than learning that needs three keys, and..." There was a moment of silence. "From the look of the book when I got it, I'd honestly say it hadn't been opened in years. Enough to wonder if the government department, whichever one it might be, actually has all three of the keys."

"You think one is missing?"

"It's more I think Uncle Tim had a reason for taking the book. He, I'm almost certain, probably has the first key, and he took it to make it impossible for them to open the book without him. When they found the other two keys, it's likely they were willing to do whatever they had to do in order to get the key he took."

"So he took the book, to make it impossible for them to open it, before starting the hunt for the other two keys."

"Leading us to where we are now. We have a book this department wants, and we already know they're watching us closely. All it takes is one mistake for us to be in the same position Paul is. We have limited options right now." Their eyes met. "We're going to need somewhere to hide. However, I'm not certain I'm willing to trust Uncle Tim the way Paul did."

"Paul might have been lying to us about the one key, assuming we wouldn't notice anything more."

Rebecca nodded. "It's also possible Tim didn't tell him the book needed more than one key, and Paul had no reason not to trust him." She looked at the book. "I don't know which it is, but we do need to put our own safety first, which to me means finding somewhere we can hide with the book if anything bad does happen."

"Hopefully, we have time. Paul was able to hide the book from them for two months. Finding somewhere will likely be a task of weeks rather than months, and for now, they have no idea any of us have the book."

"They do know we were at McKaulkin storage. They're going to want to know what we were doing there, so I don't think we have much time at all."

***

"Okay, I can do that." Sam sounded almost relieved. "I'd got to the point where I was feeling a little useless."

"Sam..."

"We all need something to do, and this can be my thing. I know there were rumors about a bunker being built locally, back when people were worried about the possibility of there being nuclear war, so finding that would be a step in the right direction."

Ben nodded. "Yeah, we do." His job, apparently, was planning, so that was what he was doing. "We're also going to need to think about what to take with us if something does happen."

"Anything preserved will be best."

"David suggested buying military supplies when I told him about what we might need to do, which isn't something I plan on doing. That's going to draw more attention than we want right now."

"How dangerous do you think this is going to become?"

"I don't know. I wish I did, but for right now, I think we need to make the most of the quiet. We know they're after the book, and Paul, while Becca thinks they're probably on the hunt for Tim too. There are three locks on the book. She believes Tim probably has one of those keys. Now he needs the other two to open the book."

"Paul trusted him."

"Yes, Paul did, but we aren't Paul. We've never met Tim, and for now, I don't think we have a reason to trust someone we haven't met. I trust the four of you. One way or another, we'll make this work." Ben smiled. "I trust Becca when she says we should be wary because she often sees things we don't."

"So do I." Sam sighed. "Anything else you need from me?"

"Not for now." Ben bit down on his bottom lip. "Are you sure you're okay with this?"

"As okay as I can be, Ben. This... it's not what any of us wanted. Finding the book was real, and now we're dealing with a government department possibly following us, was something we all kinda thought was impossible."

"Yeah, I know. I wish there was something I could do to change this."

"We made the decision knowing it was possible we'd find ourselves in this position. It's going to take some time to get used to."

"Be careful. We don't want anyone to learn what we're doing. The more we keep to ourselves, the safer we're going to be."

"I know. Don't worry about me. I'll be careful because I don't want them knocking on my door. Fortunately, I'm low down the list like Becca. You'll be the first one they want to ask questions of."

"Unfortunately. The tapes are with Becca now, so they're safe if someone does knock on the door, but I have a feeling they're going to keep watching us for a while longer. They don't want to make their move before they're truly ready because we're only Paul's friends."

***

Stepping out the door, Ben was unable to ignore the car on the other side of the road. Knowing it was there led to him looking at it every time he left the house. Fortunately, he was able to make it seem relatively natural, his eyes going over all the cars along that side, looking like he was thinking about something else entirely.

Technically he was. Ben's mind was more on what they might need if they did need to spend some time hiding out from this government department, something they still knew next to nothing about. David was digging, but trying to find the answers to the questions they hadn't figured out was going to take time, especially as he was being careful. They didn't need him getting caught like Paul was.

A list was the first place to start. Ben raked a hand through his hair. It was more than food they needed. Every one of the group needed a bag ready for if they needed to leave unexpectedly, with the changes of clothes they were obviously going to need, although there was only so much they could take with them. Walking down the street, he did his best to ignore the sound of footsteps behind him. It wasn't anything more than someone else going in the same direction he was.

Food, and water, were the next things. Maybe weapons. Should they take weapons? Would it draw more attention to them than they wanted? It seemed likely they would unless they were able to get hold of them from someone they knew. Ben shook his head. That was a question to ask the others when they were back together.

Crossing the road gave Ben a chance to see who was following him. He recognized the woman from the car. They'd made the decision they did need to follow him around. Did they know about the book? There was a chance they might have already started to suspect, but they couldn't know. It wouldn't be until they actually asked the question, and they weren't going to do that yet, still waiting to see if Paul returned.

Heading to David's was normal for a Saturday, before or after Paul's disappearance. The longer they acted normally, the better off they were going to be. As Ben walked down streets he'd walked multiple times in the past; he listened to the footsteps. Had Paul dealt with the same thing? Being alone definitely seemed worse than the group all working together.

Reaching the house, Ben rang the doorbell. Tracey answered, giving him a smile. Also, not unusual. As he stepped into the house, their eyes met for a moment. She was doing the same thing he had. They were acting entirely normal because it was the most logical thing to do. Otherwise, they'd draw more attention than they already had on them.

When the door was closed, they both let out a breath Ben hadn't even realized he was holding. "Hey."

"Hey." Tracey smiled a true smile rather than the fake one from before. "You okay?"

"As okay as I can be." His eyes met with hers. "I wanted to ask for your help."

"Planning out what happens when they inevitably start asking us questions about the book?"

Ben nodded. "Sam's looking for a place for us to go. I've been thinking about food and other supplies, along with the clothes we're going to want to take with us."

"Not going with Dave's suggestion?"

"Military supplies will draw more attention than normal groceries. If we're lucky, this won't take as long as we fear it will, and if it does, it won't be impossible for us to get what we need."

"I agree with you. We want to be making the most logical choices possible, even though nothing about this feels real yet. It's like I'll wake up tomorrow, and this will all have been a dream."

"Wishful thinking."

"Pretty much." She shrugged. "I take it you want to be using my car to start gathering everything we need."

"You're only one with a car."

"Fortunately, one of us does, otherwise we'd be in a very different position right now." She gestured for Ben to follow her. "Mom's been talking to me about getting a different car; I think she's planning for college, so I think now might be the time to go with it. Even if we don't need it now, then I can use it for the move to college."

CHAPTER 8

Gathering the bags, Ben walked toward the door of the store. Offering to get groceries for home was the best way of slipping in a few extras, and he knew the others were doing the same. It also gave him a chance to stop thinking for a while. Thinking too much only made things more complicated. His sister was waiting for him, having run her own errands while he was busy.

Ben smiled at Sarah. She smiled back, grabbing a couple of bags off him. "Get everything Mom wanted?"

"Of course." They headed for the exit, and Ben ignored the woman who'd followed him all the way around the store. "She's very particular with her lists."

"Sounds like Mom."

"Get everything sorted?"

"Pretty much." Sarah looked at Ben. "How are you doing? I know things have been hard, with Paul disappearing. This seems like one of the many ways you've been trying to distract yourself."

Nodding, Ben sighed. "In a way, it is. I thought this would get easier as time passed, the pain would fade, and I'd stop thinking about him every day, but so far, everything is the same way it always was."

"Although Paul isn't dead, you are grieving." Sarah pressed the button on her key, and the car unlocked. "It's made harder by the fact you are in classes you used to share with him every day. If that wasn't affecting you, I'd be far more worried." She opened the trunk, putting the bags she carried in. "Next year, when you aren't in those same classes, it should become a little easier."

"Maybe." Ben put the bags in the trunk with the others, and Sarah closed the trunk. "What do you think happened?"

"Honestly, Ben, I have no idea. I wish I could say something to put your mind at ease, but that's not possible. As the police haven't found a body, you could see it was a good sign that he's out there somewhere, even if it means accepting he probably left of his own accord. Someone doing that was likely hiding how much they were struggling with life for a long time."

"Do you believe he was struggling?"

"I noticed there was a distance. You were his best friend, but he kept you at arm's length for a couple of weeks, which points to something unusual happening." Sarah's eyes met with Ben's. "I know you want answers. If he was my friend, I'd want them too. I truly believe the police are doing their best to find him."

"So do I." His words were the truth, for a different reason to the one Sarah would assume. Paul was wanted by a government agency, so the police were doing everything they could, and it was one of the reasons he was almost certain they'd never find him. "Maybe one day he will come home."

Sarah wrapped an arm around Ben's shoulders. "Maybe he will. I hope he does."

He did the same to her, giving her a sideways hug which had become normal for them when he was younger and more stupid. Then they released each other, going to get in the car, giving Ben a chance to notice his stalker, who had been watching them the whole time. It wasn't a surprise. She seemed always to be there like she was waiting for him to say the wrong thing. Did she think he had some idea of where Paul was?

Climbing into the car, Ben pulled his seat belt on. They drove home in companionable silence. Sarah had no idea he was watching the car following them in the rearview. When they reached the house, they parked where they always did as Sarah pulled onto the drive. She got out the car first, Ben followed, glancing at the car once more.

"Yeah, I know." Blinking, Ben looked at Sarah. "It's been there since a couple of days after Paul disappeared, and I'm almost certain it's plain-clothed detectives watching to see if you get any contact because you were his best friend."

"A best friend he barely spoke to for two months before he disappeared." Ben shrugged, turning his attention to the trunk. "If they think he'd come to me, they're very wrong. He made his choices back then, and they didn't include me."

"Ben…"

"I'm not angry. He was obviously going through something. I just wish he trusted me enough to talk to me."

***

The phone sat on the bed, windows closed, the call between all five of them. "According to what I've learnt so far, there are at least a couple of hidden government departments, one of which I found Timothy Jackson's name connected to. I can't tell you yet what the department does. There are layers upon layers of encryption, which isn't a surprise. I was expecting this to be complicated. I'm just sorry I don't have anything more for you."

"We probably have a little while longer before anyone starts asking questions, but I don't think there will be much more time. Paul has been missing for two months and three weeks. They'll probably make a move around the three-month mark." Rebecca's voice was more informative than worried. "One way or another, they want answers to their questions, and we have no reason to believe they're going to accept we don't know anything."

"Especially as we do know something." Ben bit down on his bottom lip. "We're mostly ready if it does happen. Sam found a place, Tracey has the supplies in her new car, and Becca's keeping everything else safe. I think we have enough to keep us going until David manages to find a way to hack us the information we need."

"As long as wherever we are has Internet access. I can't hack into a government site without the Internet, and going to sit in a cafe to get access doesn't seem like the safest option, considering what we know."

Ben nodded. "Sam?"

"I have no idea whether or not there is, but we should be able to find a way to make it possible. We're going to be in a bunker. Nothing about this is going to be easy, David, and I went for the safest place I could find for all of us."

"Yeah, we can. I'm not saying that. What I need is to know, so I can prepare. As you don't know, that gives me a place to start." David's voice was calm. "I'm not angry with you for not being able to find somewhere we can use. This... it's a lot of weight on all our shoulders. We're all feeling it, especially me. Getting into government sites isn't the easiest task."

"Don't worry about how long it takes. You can't force it." Ben wished he could be there to look at David, to reassure his friend face to face. Forcing it is how we end up with them knowing far more than we want them to, so we need to make the best choices we can right now, and if that means taking this part slowly, then slowly it is. We need you, David. Losing you is something we can't deal with."

"Nothing to worry about there. I'm not going to do anything stupid. I know what I need to do next."

"From what I can see, Dave's nearly through the next layer of encryption, which will give us a little more knowledge than we had before." Tracey sighed. "I don't know much about any of this. All I do is keep an eye on things to make sure nothing untoward happens when Dave is busy."

"There have been a couple of times when I thought I was going to get caught. Fortunately, it didn't happen."

"Good." Ben's eyes stayed on the phone. "How are things with the book, Becca?"

"At the moment, it's under the bed collecting dust. I've been looking into possibilities relating to where it's come from, focusing on historical artefacts that are currently missing. So far, I haven't got anywhere, something I was expecting, but it gives me something to do while we're waiting on whatever happens next.

E.B. Jaxs

"Of course, I have got to the point where I have a couple of theories. Looking at them, seeing what they're supposed to be, it's possible we might be looking at a government department who've been taking religious artefacts in the belief they might be able to use them. The other option, as expected, is your traditional aliens, with the department being tasked to hide the truth from everyone."

"Like always." Ben smiled for a second, but it faded quickly. "What do we think it might be?"

"Probably the aliens." Tracey sounded amused. "It's always the aliens."

"When it comes to the government hiding the truth, I wouldn't be surprised if they did hide aliens from us if they did exist." It was possible to see David's expression as he spoke, even with him being on the other end of the phone. "Especially if those aliens happen to be a danger to us."

***

Focusing on homework wasn't possible when Ben's mind kept turning to the possibility of aliens. Was the book an alien artefact? Was it a historical artefact? Did the department searching for it have any idea what it was they were looking for? It seemed possible they didn't if Rebecca was right about it having never been opened.

With no one Ben could ask questions, he did his best to focus on what needed to be done. He had plenty to get done. Homework hadn't been a priority for too long, and there was only so long the teachers were going to be understanding. Grades dropping on top of everything else was going to lead to people, his parents, worrying about him more than they already did, something he definitely didn't need.

Breathing deeply, Ben studied the page in front of him. Disappearing, with the others, was going to have an effect on them and on Sarah. If there was any other option, he'd have grabbed it with both hands, but there wasn't one. Not with what they knew. The book had to be kept hidden from the government department looking for it. Had they been more open, there might've been a chance he would've been more willing to hear them out. Keeping secrets wasn't the best choice for them to make if they wanted people to help them.

Math had always been Ben's nemesis, and it was no different when he wasn't able to focus. Sarah walked into the room as he was tapping his pen on the table, glaring at the book in front of him, looking like he really was actively working on it. She grinned, stepping over to take the seat opposite him.

"Need a hand?"

"I need Math not to be so complicated."

Sarah laughed. "What you need is a teacher who can explain it to you in a way you understand, which is something I've always been good at." Their eyes met. "What are you working on?"

Knowing she was right, Ben turned the book to face her, and Sarah looked down at it. She raised an eyebrow. "I don't get it, and I never have."

"Understandable because I struggled with this." She ran her tongue over her bottom lip. "Okay, give me a minute to work out where to start. Unlike your teachers, I know how your strange brain works, Ben, so we should be able to make this a little easier for you."

"Hopefully. My grades aren't the best right now."

"No one's expecting them to be. You've been through a lot. Give yourself time to work through all of this rather than pushing yourself. You've got time to bring those grades back up if you really want to go to college, which was something you said before you weren't certain about. If you want to do something else instead, Mom and Dad would understand."

CHAPTER 9

Ben opened the door to find the woman who'd been following him on the other side, alongside the man who almost always drove the car. Slowly, breathing deeply, Ben looked between the two of them. "Mr. Crowfield, I was hoping you might have some time to talk to us." She smiled, pulling something from her pocket. "I'm Agent Jenkins, and this is Agent Free. We wanted to ask you a few questions about your missing friend, Paul Hutchinson, in the hope we might be able to find him."

"You could have done that months ago." Ben stepped back to let them in, knowing better than to say no. At the same time, he tapped letters into his phone, sending a message to Rebecca, who'd then pass it on to the others. "He's been missing for three months now, and you made the decision this was the best time to talk to me."

"We understand your anger." Agent Free's voice was sympathetic. "Before we could talk to you, we needed a chance to work through some leads we had, but so far, we've got nowhere looking for him. According to our records, you're his best friend."

"I was, for a long time." Ben shrugged. "Then Paul started to disconnect from all of us, and he barely spoke to me for about two months before he disappeared. I have no idea how much help I could be."

"Honestly, you'd be surprised." Agent Jenkins smiled. "How about we take a seat somewhere, and we can start working through the questions we have for you?"

"Questions you didn't want the rest of my family to hear?"

"Pretty much. We hate dragging people into this kind of thing for no reason, even those who were close friends of the missing because sometimes it's possible for us to find them without needing to disrupt any lives. For now, you're the only person we're planning on talking to. If you give us a reason to, then we might ask some of your other friends to clarify what you know, but this is a painful time.

"Both of us have been through something similar in the past. People we cared about disappeared. That's why we made the decision to help find Paul, as we understand how hard it is, and we wouldn't want to believe there wasn't someone out there searching for them. There's always a chance they might be found."

Nodding, Ben gestured for them to sit at the table. "Should I be answering these questions without a lawyer?"

"You aren't under any kind of suspicion. We know you didn't have anything to do with what happened to Paul." Agent Free's eyes met with Ben's. "However, there is a chance you might know something you didn't realize you knew, which will point us in the right direction. There is a chance he might be in danger, as we believe he has a family connection to someone we've been investigating, but they also disappeared around the same time Paul did."

Obviously, that was Tim. Slowly, looking thoughtful, Ben nodded again. "I don't know much about Paul's extended family, although I did know his parents relatively well. It's different now. We don't have the same kind of relationship as before."

Agent Jenkins pulled a notebook out of her pocket. "So he never mentioned anything to you about an Uncle Tim?"

"Nope, not a word." Fortunately, that wasn't a lie. He'd never said anything to them about Uncle Tim personally. "As I said, I didn't know much about the rest of his family. Regina did once mention a workaholic brother, but it wasn't in any kind of detail. From the sounds of things, they weren't close to each other."

"From what we learnt, that does appear to be the case. We do have phone records that show a number of calls between Paul and a number we believe are connected to Tim, although the name used for it was Michael Jackson. Did Paul ever mention that name?"

"I don't remember it ever happening."

"Okay." Agent Jenkins kept writing. "Did he mention either of those people to your other friends?"

"Not that I know of, Agent Jenkins, but it's not something we'd have talked about. To be honest, if he was getting to know this uncle before he disappeared, it might explain what happened."

Agent Free studied Ben. "You said he disconnected from all of you. When did it start?"

"Late November." Ben raked a hand through his hair. "At first, it wasn't really something I paid too much attention to until it got to the point where Paul wasn't spending time with anyone. Then we started asking each other what might have happened if any of us might have said or done anything to affect the relationship we had, but there was nothing any of us could think of."

"Whenever any of us contacted him, it was more normal for him not to respond than it was for us actually to hear from him. There were a few messages we got, the occasional apology for being so busy, but it wasn't anything like it had been before. We still got together on weekends, worked together on projects, ate together at lunch, and did our best not to let our friendship die because he'd walked away. Paul barely even spoke to us in class when we tried to start conversations with him."

"You'd been friends since kindergarten, right?"

Running his tongue over his bottom lip Ben nodded. Reliving it all was harder than he expected it to be. "Paul and I met on the first day. I can't tell you exactly how we became friends - I think it just happened. We talked shared pencils, and by the time we reached school, he was the person I thought of as my best friend. We stayed that way until everything changed during this school year."

"Something you never expected would happen?"

"Why would I? To me, everything was the way it had always been. Paul was the one who acted differently. The friend I'd had was gone, and I didn't quite know how to deal with it. When he disappeared...." Ben looked down at the table. "Even with how things had worked out, I didn't imagine he'd leave us all behind."

As Ben looked up again, the two Agents shared a look. Agent Jenkins turned to Ben again. "You think he made the decision to leave?"

"I think it's more I'd prefer if he made the decision to leave." Ben sighed. "At least then I wouldn't need to worry his body was going to be found. If he made the choice, then there's a chance I might see him again in the future, and I can't lose hope that's a possibility. Even with how things were, I still see him as my best friend. When I'm at school, I notice he's not there. Every time I look at where he used to sit, I can't help thinking about where he might be."

"Yet I don't know why he would have gone. The very thought... it's not like Paul. Then again, it wasn't like Paul to ignore us all for months, so I have no idea about any of this. I could be wrong. I could simply be thinking of the person I thought I knew rather than the person he became. I didn't know him well."

"Did you notice anything else unusual, Ben? The fact he disconnected from your friend group wasn't like Paul, was it?"

"No, it wasn't. I can't think of anything else off the top of my head. His choice seems to have been to keep us out of whatever he was doing. If there was anything he was involved in, he wouldn't have talked to any of us about it."

"Okay." Agent Jenkins tapped her pen on the table. "Before he disconnected, he didn't mention anything either?" Ben shook his head again without saying anything. "Was it a sudden change? One day everything was normal; the next day, he wasn't speaking to you? Or was it more gradual?"

"For me, it was sudden. The others might have noticed it more gradually, but with us, it was a case of him being entirely normal one day, and then the next, he wasn't returning any of my texts. We'd planned to spend the day together, so not getting any responses from him was unusual. I thought he was sick.

Instead, it turned out he was with someone else, although he never told me who. It could have been the uncle you mentioned."

"That helps. Do you remember the date?"

"November 21st." Ben raked a hand through his hair. "Did you need anything more? I just... it's a lot to go through all of this."

"Everything you've told us will be very useful." The two Agents stood, with Agent Free holding out a card. "If you think of anything else, then let us know. We will do anything we can to find him."

Standing himself, Ben took the card before leading them to the front door once more. "I don't believe I will think of anything, but I'll call if I do."

"We'd appreciate it." Agent Jenkins stepped out the door. "Thank you for your time. It was very helpful."

Once Ben had the door closed, he headed straight for the bathroom, where he turned the tap on, just in case. Having the table bugged was likely to be something that only happened in movies, but he wasn't going to assume one way or another, especially as he knew they needed to leave. The moment the Agents started asking questions was the moment things were going to start getting complicated.

Rebecca answered before her phone rang twice. "Everyone's ready when you are. When I got the text, I knew we needed to go when you called."

"All they did was ask about Paul. We could be worried about nothing."

"Yeah, we could, but it's better for us to make a move than it is for us to wait around." She breathed in deeply. "I'm the one with the book, Ben. This... I don't want to wait around. If they learn, I have it..."

"We're taking this all at face value. Paul wanted us to get the book, so we did, but what if we're wrong?"

"We aren't. David's found enough for us to be certain of that. He'll update you in the car."

David knowing more would help. Ben nodded. "If you're certain this is the only option, then fine."

"For now, I am. If we can learn more, find out what we learnt wasn't as bad as I think it is, then we can change tactics, but for now, what I've learnt points to us needing to leave now. They start poking around more, trying to find where Paul might have hidden the book; we might easily get to the point where we don't have a chance to leave. Now is the best possible moment we have."

"I'll grab my things. Mom and Dad will accept the note I left them, at least until I don't come back Sunday night. Then they're going to be looking for me."

"Same with all of us. I wish things were different, Ben. Leaving my parents behind isn't something I want to do either, but we have very few options, especially if we do want to learn the truth about the book."

Turning off the water, Ben headed upstairs to where his already packed bag was waiting. "Let me know when you're outside, and I'll be ready." He smiled. "It'll be good to spend some time together."

"With everything we've been through up to this point, a couple of nights camping will do us good." Rebecca knew exactly what he was doing. "See you soon."

As she hung up, Ben went through his bag one last time, double-checking he had everything. Then he went to wait downstairs. The Agents were still outside, watching the house. It wasn't as though they were going to be anywhere else, and they likely already knew they were all gathering together. Tracey's job was to make sure they couldn't be followed.

CHAPTER 10

Reaching the edge of town, right when they were the most worried about being followed, Ben glanced in the rearview mirror. Nothing. He smiled, reaching forward to put a hand on Tracey's shoulder. "We're good. Let's get going to this bunker Sam found, and we can start getting settled into our new home for the foreseeable future."

Nodding, Tracey started driving, using the directions Sam gave her. Ben found his attention drawn to the book again. Rebecca had it on her lap, hands resting on it, and he looked at her for a second, seeing the tiredness in her eyes. "I haven't slept much since we found the book. I don't know if it was the book itself or the anxiety keeping me up, but it's been a problem. Mom, fortunately, accepted the insomnia explanation."

"I'm sorry."

"Don't be. I made the decision to watch over it." She put a hand on his arm. "It'll be nice not to have to worry every day about the wrong person finding it while I'm at school. We'll all be together in the bunker, with the book."

"Yeah, I know you did, but I could have talked you out of it. Taken the weight of it on myself. Paul was my best friend, Becca."

"He was, which was exactly why you didn't have it. We have no way of knowing whether or not the Agents who visited you had some way of finding the book if it was there."

"Becca's right. The book might have some kind of power, enough that it could be found by the wrong person, and our task is the protect it." David's eyes met Ben's in the rearview mirror. "From what little I've managed to find out, this group are ruthless. They're willing to kill anyone who might get in their way, which is likely the reason Paul ran for his life. Now we have to do the same thing, in order to keep the book safe, until we know whether or not this government department should have access to it."

"Who are we to make a choice?"

"The ones who currently have it." David sounded amused. "Maybe we are the right people to make a decision of this magnitude, Ben, but that doesn't mean they are either. We're in an interesting position."

Raking a hand through his hair, Ben looked at the book. "First thing we learn more about the department, and then we make the decision. If they are the right people to have it, we give it to them."

"After talking to them, do you believe they are?"

"Neither of the Agents gave me any reason to think they weren't. Of course, it was the first meeting, and they have been watching us for months, so I have no idea what they might really be like."

"Exactly the problem." Rebecca sighed. "We don't know who they are. There's a chance those two agents are good people, the kind we can trust, but there's an equal chance they're the kind of people who want power more than anything else. If we had time, I'd say get to know them, but we don't. Right now, we have the book in our hands. It's what they're looking for. It's something Paul chose to hide from them. Yes, we have no idea what Tim's like either, but right now, I'm choosing to trust Paul over everything else."

"We all are." Sam glanced at Ben. "We don't have any other option right now. There's no way to ask him what he believes is the right thing to do because he isn't here. Our task is to make the right choice, and, for now, that seems to be protecting the book at all costs. Hence the decisions we've all made."

Ben nodded, eyes on the book once more. "I know you're right. I think talking to the Agents didn't explain why it was someone that might have taken the book from them, but Paul had to have a reason he believed in. He'd not the kind of person who'd have made the choices he did for no reason."

"Fortunately, we all know that." David smiled. "That's why we're here, doing what needs to be done."

***

Pulling the car to a stop underneath some trees, Tracey looked back at Sam. "You sure this is the place?"

"It's a bunker, Trace." He grinned. "We should be able to find the entrance somewhere nearby after we've taken the time to get everything out and hide the car."

Tracey bit her bottom lip. "Mom's going to be annoyed if I return home with the car in a state."

"We'll do everything we can to make sure that won't happen." Ben got out of the car, and Rebecca followed him, arms tightly around the book. "Becca, you look for the entrance. Get the book in there sooner rather than later. We can handle the unpacking."

"Okay." There was a flash of relief in her eyes. "Call me if you need anything, and I'll let you know when I've found the bunker."

Ben watched her for a few seconds. Hopefully, it would be a night when she could sleep because they'd all be there to watch over the book, rather than her having to worry alone. Then he turned his attention to everything they managed to get in the car. It seemed impossible, but they'd got enough food for at least a month. By then, it was possible they'd already know what their next steps needed to be.

After getting out half the boxes, Ben heard Rebecca's voice. "Found the entrance. I'm going down now, and then I'll be back up to help with everything else. I'm not going to leave you guys to do everything."

"Have a look round. See if there's anything we might be able to use down there." Ben glanced at the others. "We're good with this for now."

The sound of the door opening was loud, and then they all heard Rebecca going down a ladder. Sam nodded, pulling a rope out of the trunk, looking at the boxes they'd carefully packed. "I knew we needed to be prepared for the possibility of the bunker entrance being the type it is. We can lower everything down. It won't make it easy if we need to leave quickly."

"Maybe there's another entrance we can find somewhere." Tracey shrugged. "For now, we need to get this done. If there isn't, we'll work with what we have." She hauled one of the large bottles of water out the trunk. "We can only hope whoever built it was prepared for people staying in it for a long time."

"Unfortunately, even though I checked a number of times, this is far out enough there are no images. It was one of the reasons I picked it." Sam grabbed another of the boxes. "We wanted to be somewhere we couldn't be found. This was our best option. I think it was built by someone who understood people might need to call a bunker home for a number of years."

"Even if not, we can always find somewhere else. This simply step one. From here, we get to work out the next steps."

***

David started setting up his laptop, along with everything else he'd brought. Ben looked at it, then at David, and made the logical decision to leave it in the hands of the person who knew what he was doing. They did have electricity. From the looks of things, there were a number of solar panels carefully positioned to make it possible for someone to stay down in the bunker for a time.

Sam didn't think anyone knew about it, and Rebecca confirmed that was most likely the situation from the layers of dust everywhere. She'd been the one to start cleaning up, making the place habitable, even though it wasn't the nicest of places to be. Ben raked a hand through his hair as he looked around. It was safe. That was what they needed.

"We each have a bedroom, and the book is currently in the main space with David. Looks like there's also a small kitchen we might be able to add a couple of appliances to if we do end up staying here for longer." Rebecca smiled at Ben. "I don't know how much we dare use when it comes to the electricity. Yeah, there are solar panels, but they're only useful when it's sunny, and David's going to need the most power."

"A bridge to cross if we get to it. For now, I think we're good." Ben put a hand on her shoulder. "How are you doing now?"

"I have no idea. Everything about this is weird. Mom's going to be worried about me. I hate doing this to her, and I think I'm beginning to understand how hard a decision this would have been for Paul to make."

"Knowing more will help. David will be able to put all of his time into breaking into those sites, giving us more information about the book, which will be the point we can decide what our best option is. I don't know for certain right now hiding in a bunker is the right choice, but it's better for us to be doing this right now than it is for us to be putting ourselves and our families at risk."

Rebecca nodded. "Are you trying to convince me, or you?"

"Bit of both, I think." Ben sighed, wrapping an arm around her shoulders. "I don't know how I feel either. Everything about this is us doing what we think Paul would have done without having Paul here to ask. There's a chance he might not be missing. He might be dead, and we won't find out any time soon."

"Paul wanted us to have the book. He wanted us to hide the book and to learn where the keys are. We're making his choices. He believes this is what we should be doing, probably because

Tim told him enough for him to be certain. He wouldn't have asked us to do this if he didn't accept everything he'd been told. Of course, I'd be more inclined to take it with a pinch of salt if I hadn't spent so much of my time sleeping with that book in my room.

"There's definitely something unusual about it. I can't put my finger on exactly what, but knowing it won't be under my bed tonight is a relief. All I can do is hope it'll be far enough away from me for me to have a chance of sleeping, rather than lying awake all night, trying to work out what it was. Why I felt what I did."

"You should have given it to one of us for a bit."

"Honestly, if this hadn't happened, I was going to ask Sam to take it for a while. I think he's the one who'd be less affected by it."

Ben looked at Sam. "Why do you say that?"

"He's the most grounded of us, barring maybe Tracey. The two of them were more logical about all of this than we were. I would have asked Trace, but her living with David complicated it, so Sam was the best option. He'd have been able to ignore what I couldn't."

"Ignore what?" Tracey walked up behind them. "I'm glad to hear you trusted me enough to want to ask me."

"Always." Rebecca smiled, looking at Tracey. "Just a feeling about the book."

Tracey nodded. "I feel it too. I don't know what it is, but there's definitely something. Hopefully, it's not a bad sign."

David whooped. "I think we'll find out sooner rather than later." Ben looked between them. "I have to admit I don't feel anything, but maybe there's a reason for that. One David will find out for us."